W9-CCC-489

First American Edition 2001 by Kane/Miller Book Publishers
Brooklyn, New York & La Jolla, California

First published in Japan in 1983 under the title *Tousan Maigo*
by Kaisei-sha Publishing Co., Ltd.
English translation rights arranged with Kaisei-sha Publishing Co., Ltd.
through Japan Foreign-Rights Centre

Copyright © 1983 by Taro Gomi
American text copyright © 2001 Kane/Miller Book Publishers

Library of Congress Card Number: 00-109058

Printed and bound in Singapore by Tien Wah Press Pte. Ltd.
1 2 3 4 5 6 7 8 9 10

3 1461 00137 3601

I LOST MY DAD
Taro Gomi

A CRANKY NELL BOOK

KM Kane/Miller Book Publishers
Brooklyn, New York & La Jolla, California

I was looking at the toys, when . . .

It's okay. He's over there!
That's his suit . . .

There he is! There!
That's his hat . . .

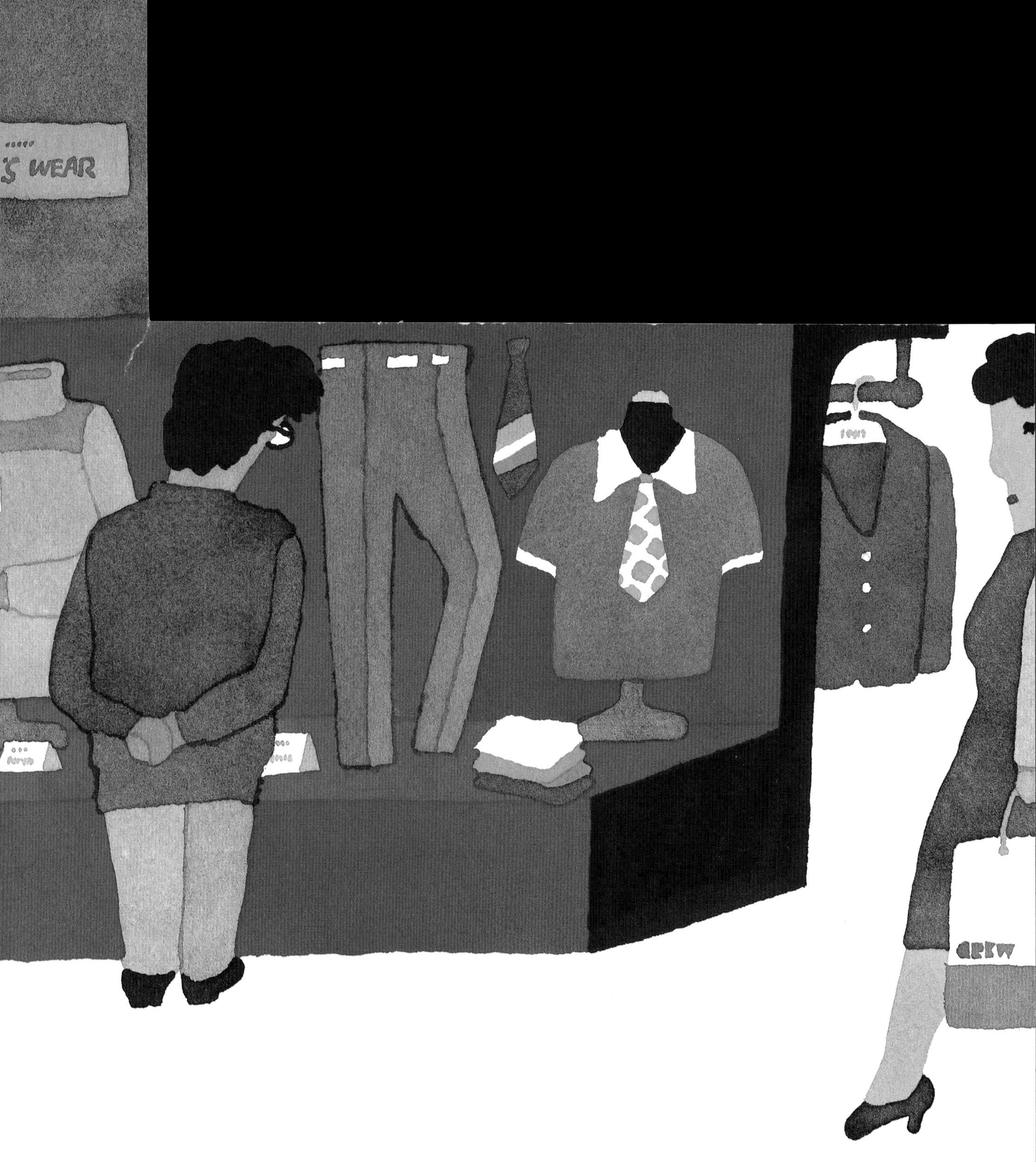
'S WEAR

No, that's not his hat.

He's there!

Those are his shoes . . .

But that's not him either.

At last! There he is! That's his tie . . .

Oh, I don't believe it!

Well . . .

Where could he be?

Son! I've been looking all over for you!
Where have you been?

I was very worried!
It's okay Dad, I found you.